The Grizzly
and the
Frigate Bird

by Susan Blackaby   illustrated by Tone Eriksen

Table of Contents

Chapter 1
The Grizzly Bear's Boast

Not so very long ago, a grizzly bear and a frigate bird lived quite happily near the sea. They liked each other's company and spent many hours talking about fishing. Both of them ate a steady diet of fresh fish, and each had a particular way of catching it. Secretly they each thought that their own special method was by far the best.

The grizzly bear lived in a cozy den hidden in the forest overlooking the ocean. She followed a path through a thicket of ferns and trees to reach the mouth of the river near the sea. During the day, especially early in the morning or just before sunset, she could be seen roaming around the river looking for fish. On warm days she spent her afternoons resting in a quiet, sandy spot where she could keep an eye on the business of the beach. From there she would watch for her friend the frigate bird, swooping in from a corner of the sky.

The frigate bird lived in a nest made from a messy jumble of twigs. It was perched high on a narrow ledge partway up the rocky cliff that rose out of the water. From there the frigate bird could fly off in all directions. He darted and dove, looping through the sky. He loved to glide for miles and miles over the open sea or skim low along the coastline, following the tide. If he spotted the grizzly bear resting in her lazy place, he would circle down to say hello and compare fishing stories.

One day the two friends were having their usual conversation and, as always, their chatter turned into a debate about the smartest way to catch fish. The grizzly bear began boasting about how no one else on earth could possibly fish quite as well as she could.

"I cannot help but say that there isn't anyone who can catch fish quite like I can," said the grizzly bear. "I snatch them right out of the water with one lightning-fast swipe of my paw. It takes a great deal of practice, as you certainly must know. I have applied myself, though. I have perfected my method, and the fish don't stand a chance."

The frigate bird listened politely, but he was not very impressed. He had heard the grizzly bear say things like this many times before. He never agreed with her ideas about scooping fish out of the water. To him it not only seemed like a lot of extra effort, it also seemed to take a huge amount of time. The grizzly bear spent hours standing in one spot, staring into the water, waiting for just the right moment to reach for a leaping, silvery fish. The frigate bird liked his method better. His way, someone else did most of the work.

"I suppose that without much practice I could easily do that myself," said the frigate bird with a bored sniff. "I just don't see the point. Only this morning I seized a fish from the beak of a pelican. I grabbed it out from under that silly bird's nose. He never knew what hit him." The frigate bird fluffed up his black feathers. "I guess some animals might call this stealing," admitted the frigate bird. "I like to think of it as a golden opportunity."

The grizzly bear sat quietly a moment, tapping her chin thoughtfully. "You know," she said at last, "I think it would be a wonderful experience if you were to come fishing with me tomorrow. We can fish together, and you will see for yourself what an expert I am. I do not need any help from a pelican. What do you say?"

The frigate bird nodded in agreement. "I would be delighted to go fishing with you," he said. He was sure that the grizzly bear couldn't be as good at fishing as she said she was. He wanted to see her in action. "I will meet you here by the river for breakfast."

Chapter 2
Fishing on the River

Early the next morning, the grizzly bear and the frigate bird met up on the rocky land at the mouth of the river that ran into the sea. The grizzly bear stood perched on a big rock overlooking the swirling waters. She looked as graceful as a ballerina standing on tiptoe.

The frigate bird always moved awkwardly on land. He would sway as he struggled to stay on his feet. Today was no different. He went hopping and flopping from rock to rock, trying to keep his balance. Several times he toppled into the water. Each time, he scrambled back up onto the rocky shore, gasping and sputtering. His waterlogged feathers made it even harder for him to move. He stumbled and slipped and slipped and stumbled.

The grizzly bear paid no attention to the frigate bird's problems. She was too busy grabbing silvery fish out of the water right and left.

By midmorning the frigate bird had had only a few bites of fish. He had to admit that the grizzly bear's fishing method was quite amazing.

"I have to say that your knack for catching fish in this river is second to none," said the frigate bird. "You can really put those fish away."

The grizzly bear patted her round, fuzzy tummy and chuckled happily. She was feeling pretty satisfied with herself. "Well, you either have it, or you don't," she said. She reached into the water, pulled out a fish, and tossed it to the frigate bird. The frigate bird caught the fish in mid-air and gobbled it down.

"I can see that you certainly do have it," said the frigate bird. He wobbled on the rocks and nearly flopped head over heels for the fifth or sixth time. "I can barely keep from tipping over, let alone scoop fish out of the water."

The grizzly bear reached out a big paw. She pulled the frigate bird upright again. The frigate bird leaned on the grizzly bear, and the two of them picked their way along the rocks.

"We must do this again very soon," said the frigate bird. "In fact, I have just now had the most fantastic idea. Why don't we try out my favorite fishing spot tomorrow?"

"That does sound like a fantastic idea," said the grizzly bear. "I will look forward to it. I will meet you at the beach first thing in the morning."

Chapter 3
Fishing on the Sea

The next morning, the frigate bird walked up the beach, tipping and tottering as usual. "Good morning," said the grizzly bear, who had been waiting patiently but was beginning to feel a little bit hungry. "I am ready for a fish-filled morning. Where is this fishing hole of yours, anyway?"

The frigate bird pointed with a dark, glossy wingtip to the ocean, stretching out to the horizon. "It is just a little ways offshore," he said. "I hope you are ready for an early dip. I can skim low over the water, and you can follow along. Do you think you can keep up with me?"

The grizzly bear was a good swimmer, and so she did not hesitate. "Of course I can," she said, and she dove into the foamy surf.

The frigate bird stumbled over the sand and then flapped his huge wings. He rose gracefully into the sky and headed westward. The grizzly bear bounced and rolled through the tumbling waves, gulping and spitting mouthfuls of seawater. She paddled out into the open water, wagging her bottom and splashing her big paws and kicking her feet. Overhead, the frigate bird glided easily. Now and then he swooped downward to check on the grizzly bear's progress. Once in a while, a passing seabird holding a slippery silver fish interrupted the frigate bird's flight. The frigate bird could not resist flying over and stealing the tasty meal away from its owner.

Meanwhile, swimming paw over paw, the grizzly bear worked to keep up with the diving, sweeping frigate bird. She could see the frigate bird spiraling off to grab fish away from every pelican or gull that happened by.

"I can't believe how easily the frigate bird swoops and dips," thought the grizzly bear. "He is hopeless on dry land. I had no idea he could fly so beautifully. That forked tail of his is just like a rudder, steering him through the sky."

The frigate bird had led the grizzly bear far out to sea. The grizzly bear was growing weary of water and swimming, and she was feeling hungrier with every stroke. She had not gotten even a single mouthful of fish for breakfast, and it was getting close to lunchtime.

The grizzly bear stopped swimming and waved her paws in the air. In a jiffy, the frigate bird flew close enough that the grizzly bear could feel the breeze from his flapping wings. The frigate bird made a slow circle over the grizzly bear's head.

"Excuse me for a moment," the grizzly bear called up to the bird. "Do you think you could snag me a fish while you are out meeting pelicans? I kind of have my paws full just staying afloat out here."

The frigate bird said, "I would be happy to oblige." He flapped away until the grizzly bear could see only a tiny speck moving across the sky. But in no time at all, the frigate bird returned and dropped a fish into the grizzly bear's jaws. She gulped it down in two bites. The frigate bird delivered three more good-sized fish to the waiting grizzly bear.

Even though she had gotten both breakfast and lunch delivered, the grizzly bear still felt hungry and was getting very tired of swimming. She splashed along for another few minutes. Then she waved to get the frigate bird's attention again.

"How much farther do we need to travel to reach your fishing spot?" she called out.

The frigate bird arced into the sky and then dove down toward the water, gliding along beside the grizzly bear.

The frigate bird smiled. "You know that I get my name from the sailing ships that skim the sea, don't you?"

The grizzly bear nodded, dipping her chin into the water.

"They call me that because I can fly over the ocean like this for days without any problem at all. About three days out from shore, a stream flows through the ocean. The current is filled with schools of fish. Plenty of pelicans are flapping about too. It is a fabulous spot. You will love it."

The grizzly bear gulped a mouthful of water. "Your fishing spot is three days away?"

"Give or take," said the frigate bird, doing figure eights over the grizzly bear's head. "With a good tailwind, I can sometimes make it in two."

The grizzly bear watched the frigate bird, swirling and dipping. "That bird could keep going for days," the grizzly bear thought, "but I certainly can't. A tailwind won't help me a bit!" She longed for her sunny beach and her nice dry den. "I am sure it is a fine fishing spot," she said, "but I didn't know it was so far away. I have things I need to do at home."

With that, the grizzly bear turned around. She raised a paw to wave goodbye to the frigate bird and then, paw over paw, started swimming for shore.

The sun was disappearing into the sea by the time the grizzly bear reached the rocky ledge. She was glad to be home and ready for a little bite of dinner before bed.

Chapter 4
Fishing Friends

A week or so later, the frigate bird met up with the grizzly bear near the beach. "I trust your fishing trip was a success. It was magnificent to watch you snapping up fish in mid-flight," said the grizzly bear.

"Why thank you," said the frigate bird. "I am sorry that the distance was too far for you to swim. Still, you are unbeatable when it comes to catching fish on the rocky ledges of the seashore."

"I know," said the grizzly bear.

The summer passed, and the two friends got together often. When the frigate bird was out fishing far and wide, the grizzly bear stayed busy around her seaside home.

One day when the frigate bird returned from fishing, he was surprised to find a tall perch built on the bank of the river. He swooped in for a landing and grabbed it with his claws.

"I can't believe this," he cried. "I can stand up on dry land without toppling over!"

The grizzly bear felt pleased. "While you were gone, I asked a carpenter to do some work. He likes to rebuild things that need repair. I asked him to add some support sticks to your nest, and he had some leftover scraps for this perch. Now you can stay on your feet, and you have an excellent view of my fishing spot."

"This is the greatest gift," the frigate bird exclaimed, hopping to the right and back to the left along the perch.

The grizzly bear tossed the frigate bird a chunk of fish. "My pleasure," she said. "He also built me a little raft so that I can join you on the high seas without so much huffing and puffing."

A few weeks later, the grizzly bear was dozing in the sunny dunes when the frigate bird came swooping in low.

"There is a school of fish heading this way," called the frigate bird. "Paddle out to the west a little way and you will see them. Follow the pelicans."

The grizzly bear jumped up, suddenly wide-awake. She hopped onto the wooden raft pulled up on the beach. The sea rolled in, and the grizzly bear pushed off and bobbed out into the ocean like a floating cork. When she reached the pelicans' fishing spot, she knelt on the edge of the raft and scooped fish out of the water. Overhead the frigate bird grabbed fish from the pelicans.

"Now this is fishing," said the frigate bird.

"That is exactly what I was going to say," the grizzly bear replied.

Not so very long ago, a grizzly bear and a frigate bird lived quite happily beside the sea. Both of them ate a steady diet of fresh fish, and both had a particular way to catch it. They liked each other's company and spent many hours talking about fishing when they got together to visit. Secretly they each thought that their own special method was by far the best.

Comprehension Check

Summarize

Use a Judgment Chart to make judgments about the actions in this story. Then summarize the story, telling why the frigate bird and the grizzly bear agreed to disagree about the best way to catch fish.

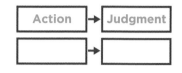

Think and Compare

1. Read the conversation between the grizzly bear and the frigate bird on pages 13-15. Do you think the frigate bird meant to trick the grizzly bear into swimming out to sea? *(Make Judgments)*

2. Have you ever been misjudged by someone who doesn't know you? What did you do to change the person's mind? *(Evaluate)*

3. What does this story teach about friendship? *(Apply)*